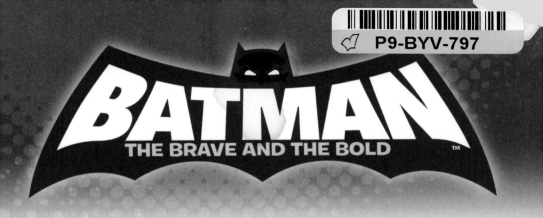

BATMAN
THE BRAVE AND THE BOLD ™

EVIL UNDER THE SEA!

adapted by Kirsten Mayer
based on the teleplay by J.M. DeMatteis
Batman created by Bob Kane

Grosset & Dunlap
An Imprint of Penguin Group (USA) Inc.

GROSSET & DUNLAP
Published by the Penguin Group
Penguin Group (USA) Inc., 375 Hudson Street, New York, New York 10014, USA
Penguin Group (Canada), 90 Eglinton Avenue East, Suite 700,
Toronto, Ontario M4P 2Y3, Canada
(a division of Pearson Penguin Canada Inc.)
Penguin Books Ltd., 80 Strand, London WC2R ORL, England
Penguin Group Ireland, 25 St. Stephen's Green, Dublin 2, Ireland
(a division of Penguin Books Ltd.)
Penguin Group (Australia), 250 Camberwell Road, Camberwell, Victoria 3124, Australia
(a division of Pearson Australia Group Pty. Ltd.)
Penguin Books India Pvt. Ltd., 11 Community Centre, Panchsheel Park,
New Delhi–110 017, India
Penguin Group (NZ), 67 Apollo Drive, Rosedale, North Shore 0632, New Zealand
(a division of Pearson New Zealand Ltd.)
Penguin Books (South Africa) (Pty.) Ltd., 24 Sturdee Avenue,
Rosebank, Johannesburg 2196, South Africa

Penguin Books Ltd., Registered Offices:
80 Strand, London WC2R ORL, England

Library of Congress Cataloging-in-Publication Data

Mayer, Kirsten.
Evil under the sea! / adapted by Kirsten Mayer ; Batman created by Bob Kane.
p. cm.
ISBN 978-0-448-45458-0 (pbk.)
I. Title.
PZ7.M4613Ev 2010
[Fic]--dc22
2009048646

ISBN 978-0-448-45458-0   10 9 8 7 6 5 4 3 2 1

CHAPTER 1

Batman flew over the Mediterranean Sea in his Batplane. The plane's radar detected an earthquake. Batman looked at his map.

"It's centered two hundred miles south. That's close to Atlantis. I'd better check that out," Batman said out loud. He pressed a button and the plane's wings folded up to transform the vehicle into the Bat-Submersible. Batma:

and his vehicle then dived into the water.

The Bat-Submersible zoomed along the ocean floor past clumps of seaweed, a shipwreck, and schools of fish. It glided over some rocks and entered Atlantis, the Kingdom of his friend Aquaman.

The majestic domed city rose from the seafloor up ahead. Batman soon spotted his friend zooming on the backs of two dolphins, with an assistant swimming behind him.

Aquaman was the King of the Seven Seas and protector of all the oceans—but sometimes even the protector needs protecting. Batman spotted a glint of light from the rocks. Looking closer, he saw a shadowy figure taking aim at his friend with an energy harpoon!

Batman quickly ejected from his Bat-Submersible. He was wearing flippers on his feet and an underwater breathing mask. The Caped Crusader tackled Aquaman, pulling him off the dolphins just in time! The harpoon swooshed past them and hit the Bat-Submersible, causing a huge explosion!

Aquaman stayed hunched over for a minute. Batman was worried. "Aquaman, are you hurt?" he asked.

Suddenly Aquaman flipped his head up and opened his arms wide. "Yes!" he shouted. "I'm hurt that you didn't tell me you were stopping by! How are you?" Then he crushed Batman in a big hug. "Hang on," Aquaman said, releasing Batman to put his fingers to his temple. He could speak to the animals in his sea kingdom through telepathic mental transmissions.

"There's someone else who wants to say 'hi,'" he told Batman.

With a chittering noise, an excited dolphin zoomed up to Batman and started nipping at his cape like a playful puppy. "It's Fluke!" cried Aquaman. "Look how excited he is! Boy, did he miss you, Batman."

Batman groaned. The dolphin was the most annoying animal he'd ever met. "Tell him to release the suit," he said through gritted teeth.

Aquaman rolled his eyes and formed a ba[ll] water that he tossed for Fluke to chase afte[r]. "He's just a dolphin, for Neptune's sake." He turned around to find his friend examining the debris from the explosion.

"Close call. Someone wants you out of the way," Batman said.

CHAPTER 2

Aquaman wasn't worried about the attack. "Happens constantly." He dismissed it with a wave of his hand. "Villains are always coming down here to take a potshot at the king fish."

As Batman picked up the mangled harpoon, a dark-haired, grim-looking man swam up to them. "What happened here, little brother?" he asked Aquaman.

"Everything's fine," said Aquaman. "Batman totally saved my seaweed."

"Orm?" Batman asked. He was surprised to see the king's brother. As far as he knew, Aquaman and his brother, Orm, were sworn enemies. They had been ever since their mother had chosen to crown Aquaman king over the older Orm.

"Big shock, I know," replied Aquaman, draping an arm around his brother's shoulders. "But we're talking again for the first time since I became king."

Orm looked at Batman.

"After my brother's coronation," he explained, "I admit pride made me do some foolish things, but age has brought me wisdom and taught me the importance of family."

Aquaman smiled. He was touched by what Orm had said. "Those years were hard on me, too," he added, squeezing his brother.

Orm freed himself from the hug and took the harpoon out of Batman's hand. "My men will look into who's responsible for this outrage. I'll see to it that nothing disturbs your party tonight, brother." Then he bowed and swam away.

Batman just looked at Aquaman.

"I know, I know," said the king. "You don't trust him."

"A tiger shark doesn't change its stripes," said Batman.

"He's family," said Aquaman.

Batman just nodded.

"Anyway," Aquaman continued, "to what do I owe the pleasure of your visit? Tell me you're joining us this evening. We're having a party to celebrate all my adventures and all twelve thousand years of Atlantean history!"

Pulling out his handheld device with the map on it, Batman explained what he had seen on

his radar. "I'm here to check out some unusual seismic activity along the shelf. If a piece came loose, Atlantis would be destroyed."

"Undersea plate movement? Happens all the time," said Aquaman with a shrug.

The ground trembled slightly, making the seaweed waver around them. "See? Still, where Batman goes, adventure follows. Mind if I tag along to check it out?"

CHAPTER 3

Aquaman liked to recount tales of all his past adventures. As he and Batman swam toward the underwater shelf, he pointed out various trophies along the way. As they passed a statue of Poseidon, he said, "I call that adventure 'The Mystery of the Stolen Statue.'" Then he pointed to a robotic monster head lying in the sand. "'The Secret of the Mechanical Sea Monster.'"

As they passed a coral reef, he said, "'Coral Reef Rescue.' Then there was the time I wore an eye patch to infiltrate a crew of pirates. I call that—"

Batman interrupted to tease his friend. "Aquaman's Undercover Adventure," he guessed.

Offended, Aquaman shook his head. "No—'The Time I Wore an Eye Patch to Infiltrate a Crew of Pirates.'"

Suddenly, a large shadow passed over them. Then another shadow appeared below them on the seafloor—and it was shaped like a shark!

"Shark attack!" cried Batman as they dodged away from the ferocious-looking shark. But the big fish swam right past them and kept going.

"No, he's fleeing something," observed Aquaman. "But what?" He found out very soon, as two narwhals with long, pointed horns and a giant sperm whale appeared, heading straight for them!

"I got this." Aquaman concentrated and tried to communicate telepathically with the animals, but they did not change their course. "Outrageous," the king exclaimed. "They're not listening!"

Before the heroes could swim out of the way, the sperm whale opened its huge mouth and sucked in a tidal wave of seawater. Batman couldn't resist the turbulent water around him and was sucked right into the belly of the whale!

CHAPTER 4

Aquaman still had two narwhals to fight off. He created a shield and sword out of water and began jousting with them. "I don't know what's gotten into you two, but you'll have to do better than that!" he cried, enjoying himself.

The two narwhals decided to charge at the same time. Aquaman shot up between them and grabbed a horn in each arm. Then he jammed their horns into the sand. The narwhals struggled, but they were stuck!

Aquaman noticed something very curious. On top of each animal's head was a tiny, black, dome-shaped device with blinking yellow lights. He removed the devices and examined them more closely. As Aquaman was checking out the strange instruments, the sperm whale approached, intending to add another hero to his meal.

"Aw, crabcakes," said Aquaman.

However, with the devices removed, the narwhals were now on their king's side. Aquaman pulled them up from the sand, and they crossed their horns in front of him, creating a shield. Aquaman nodded thank-you and then zoomed up over the sperm whale's head. Just as he had guessed, there was another device stuck to the whale.

Aquaman snatched the device from the whale and then sent a telepathic message. The whale obliged by barfing up Batman in a cloud of krill and other debris.

Aquaman slapped his friend on the shoulder. "Outrageous! What's it like inside a whale?" he asked eagerly.

"I won't be ordering calamari for a while," joked Batman as he brushed the slime off himself.

Aquaman handed one of the devices to Batman. "I found these on their heads. They told me they were overcome with the urge to attack."

Batman narrowed his eyes. "Your brother, Orm, has the same telepathic powers that you do. He may have ordered the attack and used these to block out your telepathy so that you couldn't call it off."

Aquaman's green eyes flashed. "Look, Orm left Atlantis soon after I was crowned. He drifted for years, but the prodigal brother has returned and I'm giving him a second chance."

He pointed to the device in Batman's hand. "Besides, Orm is not a genius. This is no doubt the work of my archenemy Black Manta. My brother would never hook up with him. Black Manta wants to *destroy* Atlantis. Orm loves the city as much as I do."

"What he loves is power," Batman countered, "which you would see if you weren't blinded by guilt over becoming king."

"Just drop it, old chum," Aquaman said. "Let's look at what we came here for."

Batman pulled out his device to track the location of the earthquake. "This is the spot," he confirmed. "Though I don't see anything here that would cause the disturbance."

Suddenly, Batman was spun in a circle as Fluke the dolphin swam up and nipped the device from Batman's hand.

"Fluke!" cried Aquaman. "Wow, does he like you, Batman. And he forgives you for getting crabby with him earlier." Batman grimaced as the dolphin chattered and clicked to the king. "Right, we have a party to prepare. Unless there's anything else you'd like to check out?"

Batman looked around and then shook his head reluctantly. Something didn't feel right, but he couldn't put his finger on what it was. He followed Aquaman and Fluke back to Atlantis.

CHAPTER 5

At the celebration dinner, Aquaman and his wife, Mera, sat at a grand table on a balcony overlooking all of Atlantis, where all the sea people had gathered to hear their king speak. Orm was seated next to his brother. Batman watched from behind a nearby pillar, keeping an eye out for any trouble.

The king stood and spoke to the crowd. "May

the spirit of adventure that led our people here so long ago continue to inspire Atlanteans for another twelve thousand years!" As he was speaking, Orm squeezed a few drops from a sea urchin spine into the king's goblet.

Batman didn't miss a thing. "Deadly sea urchin toxin," he whispered to himself. "Gotcha!"

As Aquaman raised the goblet to his lips in a toast, Batman tossed a Batarang. It knocked the goblet out of the king's hand as Batman leaped forward to grab Orm. The crowd gasped in shock.

Batman pinned Orm down on the table and leaned over. "Anything you'd care to confess?" he asked.

"Batman! Release my brother!" ordered Aquaman.

"But I saw him!" protested Batman.

"What? Flavor my drink? Sea urchin venom is toxic to surface people, but not to us." Aquaman demonstrated by picking up the sea urchin spine and squeezing a few drops directly into his mouth. Then he motioned two guards to come forward.

"You have to go. I like you, Batman, but this is family. You understand." Aquaman nodded at the guards. "See that Batman is escorted safely to the coast."

As Batman was led away, Orm turned to his brother. "A word in private, if I may?"

"Of course, Orm. And I'm sorry about Batman." Aquaman followed Orm into the royal fish nursery . . . headed for a big surprise!

CHAPTER 6

Orm led Aquaman into the darkened building, and paused in front of a glass wall. Behind him, fish swirled around in the water.

"I want your opinion, brother," Orm said. A large octopus appeared in the water behind him. Orm smashed the glass wall. The octopus and other sea creatures clung to his body, creating a fearsome costume.

"Does this make me look like a king?" he asked.

Aquaman was stunned and confused. "Orm . . . ?"

"A king deserves a royal name," Orm said. "You became Aquaman. Now you can call me Ocean Master." His octopus tentacles surged forward and grabbed the royal trident from Aquaman's hands.

The two brothers wrestled each other, throwing punches and grappling for the trident. Finally, Aquaman was able to grab it away from Ocean Master.

"How could you?" he shouted. "I welcomed you back with open arms! Even after all that you did!"

"I'm only taking back what's mine, brother," Ocean Master replied.

Aquaman swelled with rage and pointed the trident at Ocean Master. "I'm done apologizing for Mom's decision. She loved you, but she gave me the throne because she knew you couldn't handle the power."

Ocean Master sneered. "Then let's see how you do," he said. From the shadows behind Aquaman, two glowing eyes appeared as Black Manta stepped forward and zapped the king with an electric charge. Aquaman fell to his knees as Ocean Master grabbed the trident.

"Batman was right about you . . . and about me," groaned Aquaman.

Ocean Master laughed. "Don't expect Batman to bail you out." He nodded to Black Manta, who held up a remote and pressed a button. "Right now, your old chum is about to become fresh chum!"

CHAPTER 7

While Aquaman fought with his brother, Batman was being escorted out of Atlantean waters by two large sharks. As they swam back past the shelf, the seaweed parted to reveal large destabilizer machines attached to the rocks. Batman gasped—that's what was causing the seismic tremors! Someone *was* trying to destroy Atlantis!

Before he could do anything, though, the two sharks turned from friendly to fierce. Batman hadn't noticed the device stuck to each shark's head. When Black Manta pressed a remote control, the sharks' eyes glowed red, and they began to attack Batman.

The Caped Crusader punched the hammerhead shark on the nose, knocking it out. As the second shark swam toward him with its jaw opened wide, Batman fired a grappling rope into the shark's mouth. The shark dragged Batman along the seafloor until Batman was able to propel himself through the water and wrap the line around the shark's snout.

As the shark thrashed around to break the ropes, its tail knocked Batman's breathing mask from his face! Without air, the hero began to sink down through the water. The hammerhead shark recovered and both fish followed him, ready for a snack!

Just in time, Fluke zoomed past and hooked Batman around his fin. Then he dodged the sharks and swam past the breathing mask so Batman could grab it and put it back on. Clearing the water out of the mask, Batman began to breathe again. He patted Fluke in thanks, and

then grabbed something off his Utility Belt.

Aiming at the sharks, Batman fired an electrified net. It zapped as it surrounded the two sharks. The electricity fried the devices on their heads. As the net dropped off, the two sharks swam away unhurt.

Batman was okay, but he still had a kingdom, and a friend, to save.

CHAPTER 8

Meanwhile, Ocean Master and Black Manta had chained up Aquaman in an ancient prison cell underneath the city. A helmet was on his head to block any mental transmissions, so the king couldn't call any of his animal friends for help.

"Finally, I am king!" cried Ocean Master, holding the royal trident. "And never will I have to listen to another one of your stupid adventure stories."

Aquaman looked at his brother sadly. "Black Manta will betray you at the first opportunity," he told him.

Ocean Master smirked. "This must be where you try to turn us against each other," Ocean Master began. His voice turned into a shriek as Black Manta came up from behind and zapped Ocean Master.

Black Manta chained Ocean Master up next to his brother. "I wanted to do that within five minutes of knowing him," he said to Aquaman. "But I needed him alive to get to you. Now I can begin my endgame."

Black Manta placed a helmet on Ocean Master's head and picked up the trident for himself. "Batman's 'tremors' were tests on a series of destabilizers I set up along the continental shelf. Once started, they will collapse the shelf and Atlantis will finally be buried," Black Manta continued as he stepped out of the cell and locked the door. "Now excuse me, my lords—it's showtime."

Back at the celebration, a holographic image of Black Manta appeared overhead.

"Ladies and gentlemen," said the hologram. "Cities rise, and cities fall. Atlantis? It's going down." With a click of a button, Black Manta activated the destabilizers and cackled as his hologram faded away.

Atlanteans began to scream as huge earthquakes shook the city and the dome over their heads began to crack.

Below, in their prison cell, Aquaman and Ocean Master could feel the ground shaking. Ocean Master tried to send a telepathic message, but the helmet was blocking it. He shook his head in defeat. "It's no use."

Aquaman, however, smiled. "Where's your 'never say die' attitude, brother? Who needs telepathy?" He whistled and dozens of shrimp began crawling into the cell. The shrimp scuttled up and over the two men and picked the locks on their chains, allowing them to remove their helmets. They were free!

The two swam out of the city through a tunnel. They paused outside the dome and Aquaman looked at his brother. "Can we put our differences aside for Atlantis?" he asked.

Ocean Master took a deep breath. "Yes, sire."

They closed their eyes and used their powers to summon an army of sea creatures—whales, fish, sharks, and manta rays all heeded the call. They headed toward the continental shelf.

CHAPTER 9

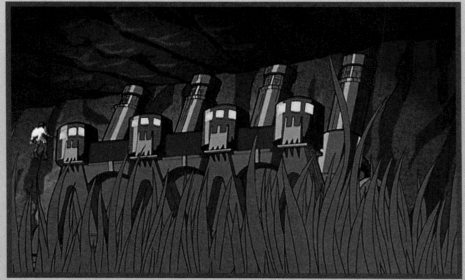

Batman managed to swim to the destabilizer machines, but so did Black Manta. The villain stood atop his destabilizer machines that were boosting giant pistons into the cliff.

"You're supposed to be fish food, Batman," said Black Manta. "Atlantis is about to be a memory and Aquaman along with it. He and his brother fell for my trap hook, line, and sinker."

"Actually," boomed Aquaman, "we're the fish that got away! En guarde!" The king and his army swam toward Black Manta. But the villain still had one trick up his sleeve. With a wave of his arm, an army of his own black-clad men appeared.

A fierce battle began. As the fish head-butted Manta's men, the villain himself aimed his electric weapon at Ocean Master and fired. Aquaman dashed to knock his brother out of the way. Surprised, Ocean Master looked up at his brother. "You saved me!"

Aaman put his hands on his hips. "I'm the It's what I do." Then he leaped straight back into battle, taking out a dozen of the enemy men.

Batman went straight for Black Manta. The two traded punches until Batman was able to knock the villain down a pit. While Batman kept the evil mastermind busy, Aquaman and his brother headed for the destabilizer machines. Aquaman threw water missiles at the pistons, while Ocean Master punched the control panel with all his might. Working together, they destroyed the machine! Atlantis was safe!

Aquaman grabbed his brother's shoulder and gave it a squeeze. "Outrageous! I knew you

had a hero inside you, looking for a way out!"

In the dark pit, Black Manta aimed the stolen trident at Batman. The hero ducked from the blast and threw Batarangs to distract Black Manta. Then he wrestled the trident away. But Black Manta wasn't finished. He still had his own electric weapon and he whipped it out to zap Batman.

Batman was just as quick and jabbed the trident right into the blast. The power of the trident forced the electric blast back at Black Manta, driving him into a wall of rock that collapsed on top of him.

"Your undersea coup is over," said Batman.

A while later, Batman went to say good-bye to his friend Aquaman. He found the king seated on a bench outside the prison cell he had locked his brother in.

"So, you decided to give him another chance," said Batman. "You could have exiled him."

"I know," said Aquaman. "But you don't give up on family." He winked at his friend and turned to his brother. "Now, where to begin?" he asked as he picked up a weighty book. Ocean Master looked nervous. He knew that the collected adventures of his brother were in that book—and that it was a *verrrrry* long book.

"Of course!" cried Aquaman. "At the beginning. 'Chapter One: A King is Born.'"

Batman smiled as he walked away.